BIGFOOT IS MISSING!

BY
J. PATRICK LEWIS
AND KENN NESBITT

ILLUSTRATED
BY MINALIMA

chronicle books · san francisco

To my little devils—Ajax, Hopper, Sanay, Selis, and Tola from Grandpat —J.P.L.

For my wonderfully weird friend, Kelly —K.N.

To my scary Brazilian creatures Marília, Ana Carolina, Lucas, Juliana, Matheus, Pedro, Alice, and Cauã —E.L.

From their (G)odd-mother to May, Joseph, Phoebe, Lara, and Molly . . . in case they haven't grown up yet —M.M.

Introduction and backmatter copyright © 2015 by J. Patrick Lewis and Kenn Nesbitt.

Poems copyright © 2015 by J. Patrick Lewis: Beast of Bodmin Moor, Ngoubou, Gambo, Dingonek, Black Shuck, Mongolian Death Worm, Goatman, Nandi Bear, Bunyip.

Poems copyright © 2015 by Kenn Nesbitt: Bigfoot, Kraken, Lusca, Lizard Man of Scape Ore Swamp, Chupacabra, Mokèlé-Mbèmbé, Loch Ness Monster, Mothman, Giant Anaconda.

Illustrations copyright © 2015 by MinaLima Ltd.

Library of Congress Cataloging-in-Publication Data:
Lewis, J. Patrick.
   [Poems. Selections]
   Bigfoot is missing! / by J. Patrick Lewis and Kenn Nesbitt ;
illustrated by MinaLima.
       pages cm
   Summary: A poetry collection about cryptozoological creatures
(the Loch Ness monster, Bigfoot, Chupacabra, etc.) from around the
world, written so as to allow the design of the book to disguise the
fact that the collection is poetry—Provided by the publisher.
   Audience: Age: 7–10.
   Audience: Grade: K to Grade 3.
   ISBN 978-1-4521-1895-6 (alk. paper)
1. Animals, Mythical—Juvenile poetry. 2. Monsters—Juvenile poetry.
[1. Animals, Mythical—Poetry.] I. Nesbitt, Kenn. II. Minalima Design
(Firm), illustrator. III. Title.

PS3562.E9465A6 2015
811.54—dc23
                  2013044354

Manufactured in China.

Art direction by Jennifer Tolo Pierce.
The illustrations in this book were rendered digitally.

10 9 8 7 6 5 4 3 2 1

Chronicle Books LLC
680 Second Street
San Francisco, California 94107

Chronicle Books—we see things differently. Become part of our community at www.chroniclekids.com.

CRYPTOZOOLOGY is the study of hidden animals, or those whose real existence has not yet been proven. Throughout the world, there are four hundred such creatures, known as cryptids, a name coined in 1983.

Though there are many alleged sightings of mysterious creatures (some more reliable than others), of course, no actual specimens or photographs have been conclusively authenticated. Hence, these creatures' existence is unconfirmed, and that's what makes them cryptids.

Are these animals real or outrageous fakes? Who knows? Still, we had enormous fun writing about them.

What would you give to see a cryptid? The only price is the coin of your imagination.

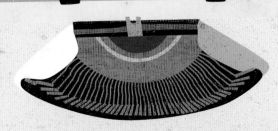

−J.P.L. and K.N.

Milk

HOMOGENIZED

Flavor Fresh

VITA...

MISSING

7'4"

LAST SEEN:
WALKING IN THE FOREST.

HEIGHT AND WEIGHT:
MUCH MORE THAN YOU.

GENDER: UNKNOWN.

HAIR: ALL OVER.

**SHOE SIZE
(RUMORED):** 92.

NGOUBOU

WHAT HAPPENED AT YESTERDAY'S JUNGLE SAFARI? LET'S JUST SAY... WE ARE VERY SORRY. —CAMEROON PARK RANGERS

YOU ARE ENTERIN PARK AT YOUR

- BEWARE OF NGOUBOU—WITH SO MANY HORNS HE'S OFTEN MISTAKEN FOR NINE UNICORNS. HE SNORTS LIKE A RHINO. NGOUBOU, THE RUNT,
- DOES NOT EVEN RUN FROM A BULL ELEPHANT!

The Davy Jones Dispatch
CLASSIFIEDS

ELECTRICAL

CHEST-TYPE DEEP FREEZER. only 1 year old. Like new!
★ SELL $175 ★
555-0101

REFRIGERATOR, 1 YEAR OLD, LIKE BRAND-NEW.
$300   555-0139

...her/Dryer, portable, ...e, white, 5 yrs old, ...OBO   555-0107

...FRIGERATOR, ...bic ft, CLEAN! ...y $150 555-0129

SAILORS NEEDED. CALL TODAY!

Last crew missing; gone aweigh. Ship leaves soon. Hard work. No slackin'. Be prepared to work with Kraken.

FURNITURE

MAHOGANY CABINET very good condition.
$40   555-0101

LEATHER COUCH 3 seater and 2 seater, good condition. $100 call 555-0182

EXTENDING TEAK DINING ROOM TABLE 6 high back chairs, matching glass cabinet, nest of 3 tables, all 3 years old. $210 call 555-0145

LARGE ASSORTMENT of old picture frames, all styles and sizes. call 555-0109

PETS

EXOTIC PARROTS available in green, red, orange, and blue. All talk on demand!
$49.99   555-0121

BABY ANGORA RABBIT female, long haired. Will require regular groomi...

CATS/KITTENS adorable rescued kittens and young cats, orange, gray, blk/white. Vetted. Fee. 555-0158

GERMAN SHEP MIX PUPS pure bred, no papers $40 only 4 left! Please call 555-0162

TENN WALKING HORSE black mare, 13 yrs, flashy, sweet...

SE...

BOOT R... for all... shoe and... repair... 555-01...

MATCHMA... Are you tire... being all alon... Looking for t... someone spec... Look no furthe... than our brand... matchmaking se... from only $30... Call Now! 555-010...

CLASSIFIED ADS
CHARGE IT.
555-0133

WANTED
OFFICE SPACE open pl...

ME: ...CCAS ...PUS, ...K). ...s

Both lizard men and cryptid spotters
enjoy our dark, unfiltered waters,
with wholesome sand and plant decay
to chase the strongest thirst away.
You'll get yours yet—it's your fate.
Cooked up since 1988.

50cl

Chapter XII

CRYPTIDS

MOST MYSTERIOUS CRYPTID

- The Dingonek, tormented brute— his tail a poison dart can shoot; his skin like an anteater's suit— is frightening.

- This "Jungle Walrus" lives on slabs of hippo, croc, before he grabs unwary fishermen he stabs like lightning.

- As Kenyan natives all suggest, disturbing his aquatic nest makes you his very welcome guest . . . forever.

- Like some newfangled dinosaur, his walrus tusks and awful roar tell you he's found a whole lot more to sever!

Fig.I-Dingonek

CHUPACABRA

^{Not} WANTED

**CRIME: REMOVING BLOOD FROM GOATS.
EVIDENCE: SMALL HOLES IN THROATS.
FEATURES: HAIRLESS. SPINY BACK.**

**GUARD YOUR LIVESTOCK FROM ATTACK!
DANGER! NOT TO BE IGNORED!**

CHUPACABRA.

👉 **BIG REWARD!**

BLACK SHUCK

WHO'S THAT SCREAMIN'?
THERE'S A DEMON
DOWN IN NORFOLK, SUFFOLK, ESSEX.
SHUCK MEANS HAIRY—
VERY, VERY—
DOWN IN NORFOLK, SUFFOLK, ESSEX.

HEARTS GROW DARK,
HE LEAVES HIS MARK.
THE DOGS MEOW AND THE
TOMCATS BARK.
MUST BE SHUCK'S AMUSEMENT PARK
IN NORFOLK, SUFFOLK, ESSEX.
RED SAUCER EYES
CAN PARALYZE
AN ENGLISHMAN OF ANY SIZE
IN NORFOLK, SUFFOLK, ESSEX.

IF YOU SEE SHUCK,
YOU'RE OUT OF LUCK,
IF HE SEES YOU, YOU RUN AMOK
IN NORFOLK, SUFFOLK, ESSEX.
AND FURTHERMOST,
THE BLACK SHUCK GHOST
CAN TURN A BODY INTO TOAST
IN NORFOLK, SUFFOLK, ESSEX
AND EVERY TOWN THAT HATES THAT HOUND
'ROUND NORFOLK, SUFFOLK, ESSEX.

MOKÈLÉ-MBÈMBÉ

DAY

B

MOKÈLÉ-MBÈMBÉ: POSSIBLE SIGHTING?

E

H

WEAKLY
Whirled News

SEE FULL STORY ON BACK PAGE

MOKÈLÉ-MBÈMBÉ EXCLUSIVE

SNAKE MAKES LAKE'S WAKES?

Here at Lake Telé, secluded in swamps, this missing celebrity privately romps. As fans and photographers hope for a sighting,

MOKÈLÉ MBÈMBÉ

prefers life in hiding.

For all the latest SPORTS results see Page 23

WARNING!
NO LIFEGUARD ON DUTY.
NO HORSING AROUND.
STAY OUT OF THE WATER
OR RISK BEING DROWNED.
NO DIVING, NO SWIMMING,
OR THINGS COULD GET MESSY.
SINCERELY, THE MANAGEMENT,
AKA "NESSIE."

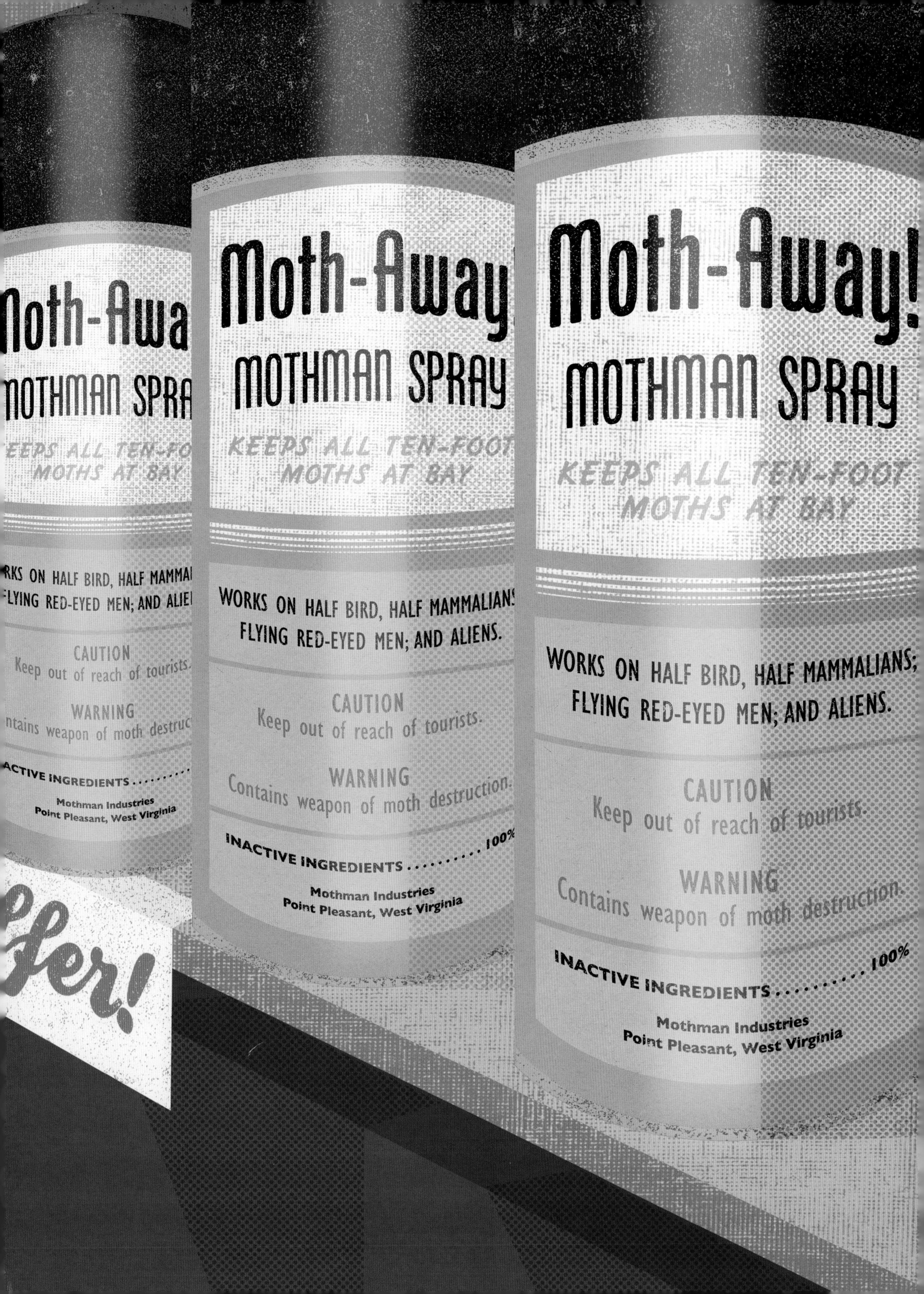

GIANT ANACONDA CROSSSSSSSSSSSSSSSSSSSSSSSSSSSSSSSSSSING

NANDI BEAR

Exhibit 7

NAMED BY THE NANDI PEOPLE OF KENYA, AFRICA
ALSO KNOWN AS NGOLOKO, DUBA, KERIT, CHIMISIT,
KIKAMBANGWE, VERE, SABROOKOO

Whose hyena laughter cracks glass
Who roars like a wounded lion
Whose shoulders mimic mountains
Who winks at the spear, scoffs at the arrow, outraces the bullet
Who pokes out his muzzle of terror after midnight
Who is said to take a human life only for its very small brain

KENYA

BUNYIP

A nightmarish fixture,
Bunyip is a mixture
of walrus, deformed horse,
orangutan.
His jaws open wide—
Avoid looking inside!
He's the opposite of the
Good Humor Man.

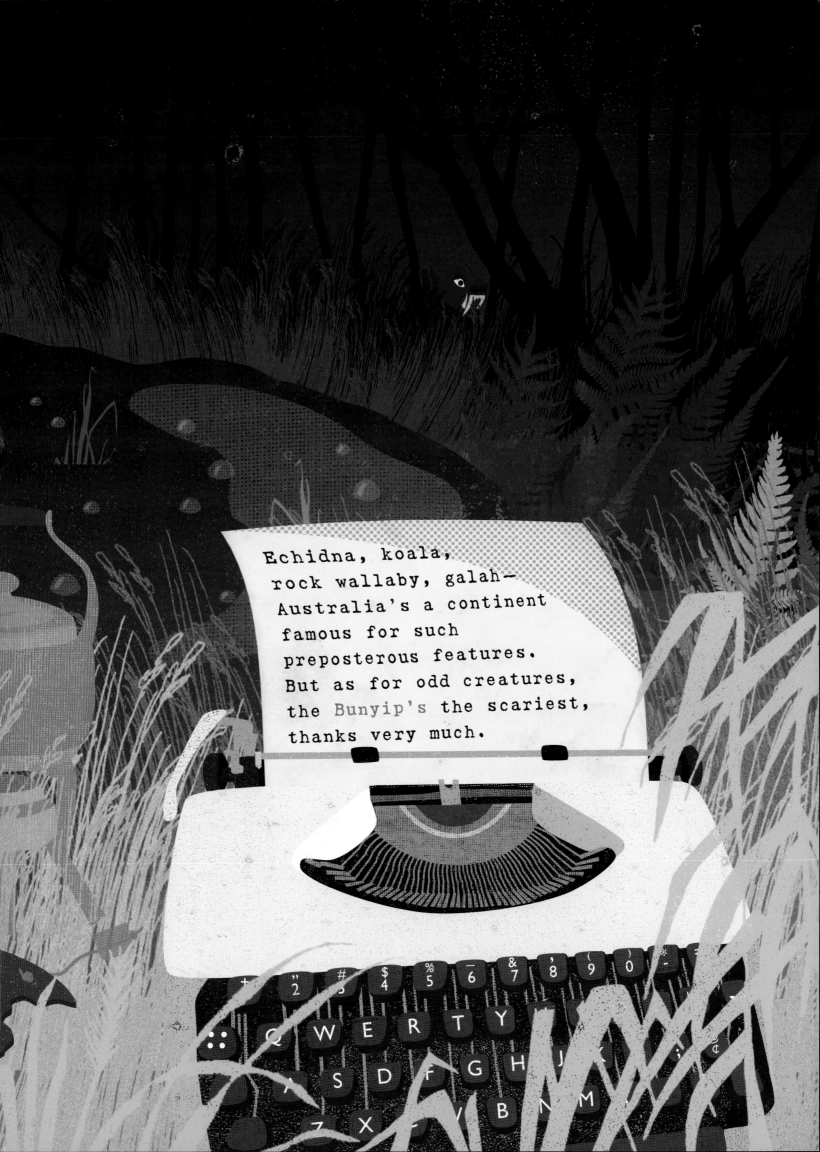

Echidna, koala,
rock wallaby, galah—
Australia's a continent
famous for such
preposterous features.
But as for odd creatures,
the Bunyip's the scariest,
thanks very much.

BEAST OF BODMIN MOOR

England

Professional naturalists dispute the existence of black wildcats in this desolate region on the basis that food is too limited and the climate is too harsh to maintain a big cat population. But beginning in 1993, residents of Cornwall have continued to report sightings and otherwise unexplained livestock mutilations.

BIGFOOT

United States of America

So named because of large footprints found near a road construction site in Northern California in 1958, Bigfoot is dismissed by most scientists as a creature of legend. However, a number of prominent scientists view the evidence as compelling, and some suggest that Bigfoot may be a descendant of a presumed-extinct giant ape called *Gigantopithecus*.

BLACK SHUCK

England

This animal, also called Old Shuck or Old Shock, is a ghostly black dog who roams the East Anglian countryside and is part of the ancient folklore of Norfolk and Suffolk. *Shuck* may come from Old English, meaning "demon," or from a regional dialect word that means "shaggy." The size of a pony or large dog, the Shuck has a loud and frightening howl, but its footsteps are silent. Some believe that the Shuck legend derives from Viking myths of Odin.

BUNYIP

Australia

First reported in the early 19th century, the Bunyip is believed to lurk in swamps and waterholes. *Bunyip*, meaning "devil" or "evil spirit," is known by many names— and as many descriptions—across Aboriginal Australia. A dreaded creature with supposed supernatural powers, it preys on the unsuspecting who encroach upon its territory.

CHUPACABRA

Central America

First reported in Puerto Rico in 1995 and subsequently in Mexico, America, and other parts of the world, the chupacabra (in Spanish, el chupacabras) is said to kill livestock, especially goats, and drink their blood. Several creatures thought to be chupacabras have been examined and found to be coyotes with severe mange. Sightings of chupacabras and reports of livestock mutilations continue.

DINGONEK

Democratic Republic of the Congo

Of all the animals discovered in Africa in the 19th and early 20th centuries, the Dingonek qualifies as the weirdest. Without actual proof, the creature remains the stuff of legend and wild speculation. Scaly, scorpion-tailed, and saber-toothed, it is said to be 12 to 18 feet (3.6 to 5.5 metres) long, with reptilian claws. The extremely territorial Dingonek lives in aquatic nests and becomes violent when disturbed.

GAMBO

Republic of The Gambia

In June 1983, teenager Owen Burnham discovered the carcass of an unidentified marine animal in The Gambia on the west coast of Africa. Locals believed it was a dolphin. The animal was about 15 feet (4.6 metres) long; its head alone was 4.5 feet (1.4 metres) long, with a 2½-foot (76-centimetre) beak. Paleontologists claimed that it was a previously unknown form of beaked whale. Gambo has also been compared to crocodiles and sea serpents.

GIANT ANACONDA

South America

Beginning with the discovery of South America by European explorers and continuing to the present, people have reported encountering anacondas as long as 60 feet (18.3 metres). While it is not uncommon for anacondas to grow to 20 feet (6.1 metres) in length and weigh more than 300 pounds (136.1 kilograms), no verifiable evidence has yet been produced of an anaconda longer than 25 feet (7.6 metres).